Millennium
The Year 2000

CHERRY GILCHRIST

Level 3

Series Editors: Andy Hopkins and Jocelyn Potter

Pearson Education Limited
Edinburgh Gate, Harlow,
Essex CM20 2JE, England
and Associated Companies throughout the world.

ISBN 0 582 43288X

First published 2000

Text copyright © Cherry Gilchrist 2000

Design by Neil Alexander
Printed in Spain by Mateu Cromo, S.A. Pinto (Madrid)

All rights reserved; no part of this publication may be reproduced, stored in a retrieval system, or transmitted in any form or by any means, electronic, mechanical, photocopying, recording or otherwise, without the prior written permission of the Publishers.

Published by Pearson Education Limited in association with
Penguin Books Ltd, both companies being subsidiaries of Pearson Plc

---

For a complete list of the titles available in the Penguin Readers series please write to your local Pearson Education office or to: Marketing Department, Penguin Longman Publishing, 5 Bentinck Street, London W1M 5RN.

contents

	pages
Introduction	iv
The New Millennium	1 - 5
The Big Step into 2000	6 - 11
Your Millennium Horoscope	12 - 15
Story in the Stars	16 - 21
Millennium Prophecies	22 - 23
Past Times, Future Times	24 - 25
The Next Millennium	26 - 29
Millennium Quiz	30 - 31
Special Events for the Year 2000	32 - 35
The Future	36 - 39
Answers	40 - 41
Activities	42 - 44

· INTRODUCTION ·

It's nearly midnight.
'Hello, Jack,' says a voice from the TV.
A woman is standing in a strange city. The buildings are round, like domes, and they are painted in unusual colours.
'You don't know me,' she says. 'I've come from the year 3000, your time. Our time is different, of course.'

As Jack watches the Millennium New Year celebrations on TV, he has a big surprise. Arindata comes from the future and tells him about life in the year 3000. She can read minds, and her people live on other planets.

As we begin a new Millennium, we think about our future. Will there be peace in the world? Will we find answers to all our problems with the environment? These are serious questions – but there is plenty to enjoy in the new Millennium too. Read your Millennium horoscope! Find out if you are ready for the new Millennium!

You can also read about events in the world at the start of the year 2000. Why were American schoolchildren writing about Mars? Where is Millennium Island, and what is the Millennium Planet? Did the Millennium Bug really make trouble? Why did people go to Antarctica on the last day of 1999? And when exactly *is* the New Millennium?

Cherry Gilchrist has written *Princess Diana, The Royal Family* and *The Streets of London* for Penguin Readers. She has also written about calendars, horoscopes, history, Russian art and many other subjects. Cherry often visits Russia but her home is in Bristol, England.

THE NEW MILLENNIUM

It was the most important date for a thousand years. Did you miss it? Of course not! If you did, you weren't living on this planet!

What do you know about times and dates?

1. What does 'millennium' mean?
   a 50 years   b 100 years   c 1,000 years

2. What language does the word come from?
   a Latin   b French   c English

3. What do we learn about from calendars?
   a Money   b Time   c Space

4. When was Jesus Christ born?
   a AD 1   b 6 BC   c We don't really know

5. Where is Greenwich?
   a In the Pacific   b In New Zealand   c In the UK

6. What is Greenwich important for?
   a Calculating international time   b Making money
   c Learning about space

7. Where can you cross the International Date Line?
   a London   b The Pacific   c The USA

8. West of the International Date Line, is the date
   a the same as the date to the east?   b one day earlier?
   c one day later?

9. In which of these places did the sun first come up in the new Millennium?
   a Australia   b Greenwich   c Kiribati

10. If it is 6 a.m. in London, what time is it in New Zealand?
    a 9 a.m.   b 6 p.m.   c Midnight

Turn to page 40 for the answers.

When does a new millennium begin?

The word 'millennium' means 'a thousand years'. We use it as part of the Christian calendar; this calendar calculates the years from the date of Jesus Christ's birth. So the year AD 1000* was the end of the first Millennium. The year AD 2000 is the end of the second Millennium, and the beginning of the third. Easy? No, not really!

First, many countries and religions have different calendars. About forty calendars are used around the world. They calculate the years from different dates, and the year also changes on a different date in each calendar.

CALENDAR	DATE
Christian	AD 2000
Chinese	4636
Indian (Saka)	1921
Islamic (Hegira)	1420
Jewish (A.M.)	5760

There is another problem too. Nobody knows exactly when Jesus Christ was born! In our year 532, a Christian man, Dionysius Exiguus, changed the Roman calendar into a new Christian one. He decided that Christ was born on 25 December, 532 years earlier. But Christ was probably born earlier than that, perhaps in about 6 BC*.

Also, Dionysius calculated in a different way. He didn't use the number 0, so there was no year 'AD 0'. But if Christ was born in AD 1, each new millennium begins in 01 too. For this reason, many people want to count the new Millennium from 1 January, 2001, not 2000.

*AD, BC: After Christ (from the Latin, Anno Domini); Before Christ

How do we calculate calendars?

People have always counted time. We want to remember when something happened in the past. And we can also predict when something is going to happen in the future. From the beginning of history, people have tried to count time from the movements of the sun, moon and stars. This way, they knew when spring was coming.

People also tried to calculate the number of days in a month and in a year from the movements of the sun and moon. But we need to put in one more day every fourth year. Without that day, spring will come later and later each year.

But our calendars also come from our gods and religions. There can be a lot of history in a calendar. In the Christian calendar, for example, people count the **years** from the birth of Jesus Christ. But the **week** is even older. People in Babylonia, more than 3,000 years ago, first chose to have seven days in the week. They named the days after their own gods. And our **months** come from the Roman calendar. But the names of the seven **days** of the week were taken from the sun and moon (Sunday, Monday) and from the old gods of Northern Europe (Woden for Wednesday and Thor for Thursday, for example).

Great periods of time

We can count bigger periods of time too. These are often part of a special view of the world. Indian Hindus believe that there are four different periods of time. Together, these periods are 12,000 years. The Greeks and Romans believed in a 'Golden Age' at the beginning of history. In this period, all men were good and wise.

A millennium, a thousand years, is another great period of

time. There is something special and important about the number 1,000. There were many prophecies about the change from the old millennium to the new one. There were predictions about the end of the world or about great changes to it. Some people were afraid, but others hoped for a new and better world – a 'New Age' of peace.

Times and dates

Greenwich, in London, is the 'home of world time'. Since October 1884, the world has used the same international time; it is calculated from the time line there. But there are different time zones in the world. When it is 3 p.m. in Greenwich, it is not 3 p.m. in every other country. A large country can have different time zones. For example, in Russia there are eleven different time zones.

The date changes by one day at the International Date Line in the Pacific. This isn't a real line – you can't see it or touch it. But the date in countries west of this line is always one day earlier than in countries east of the line.

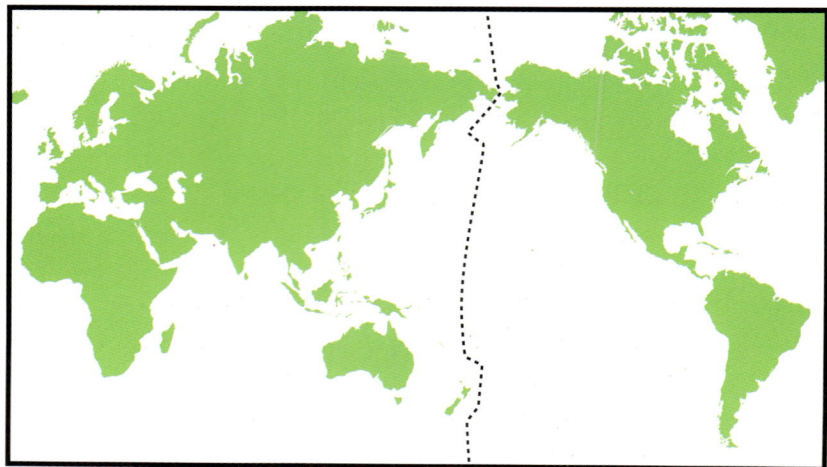

PLACE	TIME	DATE
London	3 p.m.	3 January
Japan	midnight	3/4 January
East Australia	1 a.m.	4 January
New Zealand	3 a.m.	4 January
California, USA	7 a.m.	3 January

Where did the new Millennium start?

Because of the differences in time and date, the new Millennium came to some countries earlier than to others.

• In 1995 Kiribati, a group of islands in the Pacific Ocean, changed its place from the east side of the International Date Line to the west side of the line. Kiribati wanted to be the first place on earth to welcome the new Millennium. The time difference between the different islands in Kiribati was only a few minutes.

• Kiribati dancers in grass skirts were seen on TV around the world as they celebrated the new Millennium on Caroline Island, now 'Millennium Island'. In Tonga, south of Kiribati, the government changed the clocks to a special 'summer time', so Tonga could also celebrate early.

• But who saw the first daylight of the new Millennium? In Antarctica, in January, there is daylight all the time. It was light at midnight on 31 December 1999. So some people went to Antarctica for a special Millennium party. They put on flowery shirts from Hawaii, and danced in the snow. It cost them a lot of money, but they were happy.

THE BIG STEP INTO 2000

When the world went crazy

There were parties all over the world. Many people went out into the streets. They wanted to be a part of history as it happened. Other people preferred to stay quietly at home with their families and friends.

Some of the best firework shows were in Sydney, Paris and London. In Sydney, a million people watched the fireworks over the water. About 6,000 people took out their own boats. The water was very crowded – you could walk across from boat to boat.

In Paris, mountain climbers worked for weeks to put fireworks on the Eiffel Tower. And in London, people waited all day by the River Thames to see the fireworks at midnight. They looked wonderful over famous buildings like the Houses of Parliament and Big Ben.

SPECIAL CELEBRATIONS

Israel: Two thousand white birds of peace flew up into the air in Bethlehem, the birthplace of Jesus.

Mexico: By 31 December, 1999, there were no yellow underclothes in the shops. Everybody bought them for New Year, because the colour yellow is lucky!

Spain: Thousands of people ate twelve pieces of fruit at midnight. As they ate each piece, they thought about their hopes and dreams for each month of the next year.

Scotland: In Stonehaven, a town in the north-east of Scotland, men threw balls of fire on long lines round and round their heads. In this way, they sent away bad luck and brought good luck for the Millennium.

Thailand: Four thousand people got married at the same time. The wedding cake was more than ten metres high!

People in the news at the start of the Millennium

SOUTH AFRICA

Nelson Mandela Returns to Robben Island

Nelson Mandela visited Robben Island and gave a flame of peace to a young boy. Mandela was a prisoner on the island for twenty-seven years. He wanted people to remember his fight to free black people in Africa.

Then a group of people stood in the shape of Africa and held up flames in the dark.

ALASKA, USA

Man Walks to Alaska from Patagonia

A British man, George Meegan, forty-seven, arrived in Alaska to celebrate the new Millennium. He walked there from Patagonia, in South America. The journey took him 2,425 days – more than six and a half years.

UK

British Actor Builds Millennium Dome

Rowan Atkinson is the actor who plays 'Mr Bean'. He decided to build his own Millennium Dome. It cost £50,000 and was like the Millennium Dome in London, but smaller! Atkinson invited 150 friends to a Millennium party and firework show.

Man Steals Famous Painting

A thief climbed on to the roof of a building in Oxford and cut a hole in it. Then he climbed down through the hole and stole a famous painting by the artist, Paul Cézanne. People were busy celebrating in the streets outside. So nobody saw or heard the thief because of the noise!

ISRAEL

Student Makes Millennium Clock

Yair Revivo, a student, made a Millennium clock. He lived and slept on a narrow wooden platform above a busy road for weeks before the Millennium. Every hour, he walked along the platform and changed the time on the clock. His father was worried about him and slept below on the ground. But Yair wasn't crazy. People gave him money, and he made £4,225 for his studies.

RUSSIA

President Boris Yeltsin Leaves His Job

CHINA

Thousands Watch as President Jiang Zemin Lights a Flame for a Better World

And finally . . .

NEW ZEALAND

The World's Most Boring Millennium Man

A man took his bed into the street and told his friends, 'I'm not interested in the Millennium. I'm going to sleep through all the celebrations.'

'We don't believe you can do it,' said his friends.

'Well, give me money if I can,' replied the man. 'And I'll give you money if I can't!'

The man stayed asleep all night. His friends tried hard to wake him, but they couldn't. So he won a lot of money!

THE MILLENNIUM BUG

There are different kinds of bugs. There are bugs that make you ill. There are bugs that fly. But the most famous bug in the years 1999–2000 was the Millennium Bug. It lived in computers and was also called Y2K (Year Two Thousand).

All computers use dates. But older ones use only the last two numbers, and so 00 can mean 1900 or 2000. Computer programmes can go wrong because of this. Governments and businesses were very worried. 'Planes will fall out of the sky!' said the newspapers. 'There will be no electricity! Hospitals will have to close!'

But nothing really terrible happened. Some American spy cameras in space stopped working for a few hours. Some machines in Swedish hospitals didn't work. When the lights went out in New Zealand, people were frightened. 'Is this the Bug?' they asked. But it wasn't. Somebody drank too much and knocked down some electricity lines by mistake!

COMPUTERS THAT WENT WRONG

USA: A man borrowed a video and took it back to the shop after New Year. 'It's late! That's $91,250!' they told him. On the shop's computer, it was 100 years late.

GERMANY: A bank's computer went wrong and gave a man nearly four million pounds by mistake!

CHINA: A writer lost his new book when his computer stopped working because of Y2K. What was his book about? The Millennium Bug, of course!

FIRST AND LAST

First Millennium baby	New Zealand	A boy, Tuahati Manaakitunga Edwards, was born less than a minute after midnight.
First wedding	Chatham Islands, east of New Zealand	Dean Braid, twenty-seven, a local shopkeeper, married Monique Croon, thirty-three.
First person to be 100	Australia	Violet Dickinson was born three minutes after midnight in Sydney in 1900.
Last places to celebrate the Millennium	UK	A village in Wales and an island in Scotland. They use an old calendar which was changed in Britain in 1752. New Year's Day is on 14 January.
Last people to see the sun in the new Millennium	Arctic	Workers in the Arctic didn't see the sun for weeks, because it is completely dark in winter.

YOUR MILLENNIUM HOROSCOPE

What will the new Millennium bring you? Perhaps the planets have the answer. Read your birthday horoscope.

ARIES 21 March – 20 April
You couldn't wait for the new Millennium. You love everything new. 'Old is boring!' you say. But you're running too fast into the future. Slow down a little.

TAURUS 21 April – 21 May
You like to be comfortable. Have you got enough food? Is your bed still warm? If the answer is 'yes', then you're happy. You don't mind what Millennium you're in. Look around you – life can be more exciting.

GEMINI 22 May – 21 June
You're already dreaming about the start of the next millennium – the year 3000! You'd like to move freely in time, and meet people from other planets too. But find out what you can really do. Don't just dream!

CANCER 22 June – 23 July
Did you find love at the start of the new Millennium? You're afraid of this new period of time. But if somebody agrees to walk hand in hand with you, you'll enjoy the adventure. You have a warm heart – don't hide it!

LEO 24 July – 23 August
You want to shine like the sun in the new Millennium! You want to show the world what you can do. You want to make everything bigger, brighter and better. But remember – you have to work for it. It won't just happen.

VIRGO 24 August – 23 September
You want everything to be perfect. Are you unhappy because the new Millennium isn't perfect? Don't worry too much – the world is still turning. It will never be exactly what you want. But enjoy each day as it comes.

LIBRA
24 September – 23 October
You loved all the parties and you want to celebrate the new Millennium again! Why stop enjoying yourself? You can make new friends, and celebrate life. But be serious sometimes too – there are real problems in the world.

SCORPIO
24 October – 22 November
You were secretly hoping for the end of the world. You love danger, and you were waiting for accidents. But we're still here, so now you can use all your strange ideas. Write, paint, or do something new.

SAGITTARIUS
23 November – 22 December
You know all the best Millennium jokes. You can be very funny, but you can be serious too. You're ready for this new period. Help your friends, and take them with you on the journey into the future. It's a lucky time for you!

CAPRICORN
23 December – 20 January
Old is good, new is bad. Who wants a new Millennium? Not you! But try to understand the world, and think about the future of our planet. This time is a very important part of history. So you're living through history, aren't you!

AQUARIUS
21 January – 19 February
You always like to be different. At the end of 1999, perhaps you went to a party in a tree, or under water. But don't stop there. Make some real and unusual changes in your life. Don't just talk about it – do it!

PISCES
20 February – 20 March
You don't know where you're going. But don't worry! You're swimming in a very big sea. You need time to understand this new Millennium better. You feel deeply, and other people know this.

STORY IN THE STARS

IT'S 31 DECEMBER 1999. NICKY AND INGRID ARE GETTING READY FOR A BIG MILLENNIUM PARTY.

Here, Nicky . . . do you want to borrow my jacket? It looks really good on you.

No thanks, Ingrid.

What's the matter?

It's Alex. I want to look good for him, but he doesn't notice me these days. He's too busy.

He's making plans, he says. Travel plans. He wants to go to South America next year.

It's nearly next year *now* . . . Forget about Alex tonight, Nicky. There'll be lots of other boys at the party.

But I *can't* forget about Alex. I love him.

NICKY AND INGRID ARRIVE AT THE PARTY. THEY MEET THEIR FRIEND HELEN THERE.

This is a really good party. We're going to dance all night.

Where's Alex? I can't see him.

THEN ALEX ARRIVES.

Hi, Nicky. Sorry I'm late. I've got some exciting news. I bought a ticket to South America today. At a really good price.

Oh!

NICKY SEES ANOTHER BOY, STEFAN.

INGRID NOTICES A BEAUTIFUL STRANGER AT THE PARTY. SHE ASKS HELEN ABOUT HER.

20

"Well... he went out with a girl called Lela. Don't worry, Nicky - I'm sure it's nothing. And you *were* dancing with another boy."

"Yes, but it didn't mean anything. Perhaps this is different."

HALF AN HOUR LATER.

"It's ten to twelve and Alex still hasn't come back. I must find him before the new Millennium begins."

NICKY LOOKS IN ALL THE ROOMS. AT LAST SHE FINDS ALEX AND LELA. THEY ARE SITTING TOGETHER AND TALKING.

"Nicky!"

"Er... hi, Alex. It's nearly midnight and I couldn't find you."

MILLENNIUM Prophecies

During history, people have often dreamed about a new period of time. The name 'millennium prophecy' often means a prediction for a better world, not just a prophecy for the year 2000.

A prophecy that went wrong

In the late 1900s, the Sioux Indians in North America were losing a lot of their land to white men. In 1886, Wovoka, an American Indian prophet, predicted terrible things for the white men in 1891. 'After this date, we'll get our land back,' Wovoka told his people.

Then they danced for five days at a time, to help the prophecy come true. But in 1890, white soldiers shot and killed nearly 300 Sioux men, women and children. Their new and wonderful period never came.

A new god is coming

In Peru today, a group of people are waiting for a new god to arrive. He will come down from the sky to the mountain Machu Picchu in the Andes. The old world of the South American Inca Indians will also come back to life at this time, they believe.

1999 – a year of danger!

An American, Edgar Cayce, made a prophecy in 1934. 'The world will change in 1999,' he said. 'There will be terrible accidents.'

The most famous prophet, Nostradamus, predicted terrible events for 1999. Nostradamus was born in France in 1503. His prophecies for 1999 seemed to mean that a terrible king was coming down from the sky. Did this mean a war, or a crash between the Earth and something from space? Nobody really knows. But it didn't happen in 1999!

The return of Christ

Some Christians predicted Christ's return to Earth at the start of the new Millennium. One group, 'Daystar', put cameras around the Golden Gate in Jerusalem. 'The new Christ will walk into Jerusalem on 1 January 2000,' they said. 'You can watch it on the Internet!'

'Christ will be born again in California,' said a Mr Pryor in the USA. 'He will be a girl, and her name will be Uni.'

'No, he won't,' said a group of believers in Scotland. 'He's coming to our church.' They believe that Christ's cup was hidden in one of the walls of an old church at Rosslyn near Edinburgh.

Past Times

The start of the last millennium

The world in the year AD 1000 was very different from today. People believed that the earth was the centre of everything. They thought that the sun moved round the earth. Of course, there were no cars and no computers. In Europe, people didn't drink tea or coffee, and there was no sugar. The cleanest people in England had baths only five times a year. They thought that the Danes were very strange. They had a bath once a week!

1 CHINA

To the Chinese, the world was China. They had many new things, like paper money and water clocks. They sent expensive cloth to Europe. They built a 2,500 kilometre waterway which joined five rivers. They opened the first restaurant in the world, The Chicken House, and their markets were open for twenty-four hours a day.

2 ARABIA

The religion of Islam was growing, from its birthplace in Arabia to India and Spain. Moslems were very interested in the sciences of medicine, numbers and the stars. They also helped to bring old Greek and Roman learning to other parts of the world. Cordoba, in Spain, was a Moslem city with a library of over 400,000 books.

FUTURE TIMES

3 EUROPE

Not everybody in Europe was a Christian. In Russia, for example, Christianity only arrived in AD 988. Many Christians thought that AD 1000 was the end of the world. But nothing happened. The world was still there. So they began to build many large and beautiful stone churches in Europe. It was the beginning of a New Age.

From about AD 950 to AD 1300, the weather was hotter than today. The weather and the seasons were very important. Most people kept their own animals and grew their own food. Many people killed wild animals in the forests for food too. Europe had bigger forests then, and wood was used for everything – for fires, buildings, ships, and for ordinary things like plates and cups.

People often travelled by river, because there were fewer roads. Roads were often bad, and unsafe too. They were usually on high ground above the forests, so thieves and wild animals couldn't attack travellers easily. Sometimes people went on religious journeys to special places. The first hospitals were built along these roads to help sick travellers. It was a dangerous world, and you could easily die young. A person of forty was already quite old.

But people liked to enjoy themselves too. When they had a big meal together, it was a real celebration. Not many people could read or write. But they played games, and sang, and told stories and jokes. They learned about their history, and heard beautiful poems.

The Next Millennium

It's 31 December 1999. Jack is sitting in front of the TV with a can of beer in his hand. He looks angry.

'Come out with us, Jack,' says his Mum. 'We're going to the big party in the town centre. All your friends will be there.'

'No,' says Jack rudely. 'Leave me alone. The Millennium isn't special to me. I don't want to go to a stupid party. I want to stay here.'

His parents go out and Jack switches on the TV. It's nearly midnight.

'Hello, Jack,' says a voice from the TV.

A woman is standing in a strange city. The buildings are round, like domes, and they are painted in unusual colours.

'You don't know me,' she says. 'I've come from the year 3000, your time. Our time is different, of course.'

'Is this a joke?' asks Jack.

'No. We know this is an important day for your planet. We wanted to come and tell you about the future.'

'How do you know my name?'

'We know your name because we can read your mind. My name's Arindata.'

'Where are you from? How did you get here?'

'We live on many different planets,' Arindata tells him. 'Some people still live on our first home, Planet Earth. I live on Planet Osanak. We have a lot of water there – seas and rivers. Some people like heat, so they live on drier planets.

'We've made Space Gates. They're gateways to the stars and they change time and space. So now we can travel in our spaceships as fast as we like. We can go anywhere in our world. We hope that one day we'll make a gateway into the next world. We think there are millions of other worlds.'

'Leave me alone. I want to stay here.'

'Are those domes your houses?' Jack asks.

'Yes. We can make any kind of house. And we can change them. If I say, "Put in a new room!" my house will grow a new room. It can change colour too.'

'Are you all the same?'

'People on each planet are a little different,' Arindata replies. 'For example, the people on colder planets are fatter. Each planet has its own language and religion. But there's one Government for all our World, and World Teachers too. We need to understand people from different planets.'

'Do you ever get ill?'

'When people first went into space, they got a lot of new illnesses. But now we can stop most of them. We make new parts for bodies too.'

'So you have no problems?' asks Jack.

'Of course we do! We're still people. We still love and hate. We get sad too. I'll be very sad if my nogorot dies.'

'Nogorot – what's that?'

'Sorry! It's a kind of pet. The Animal Science Farm made it for me. It's a small animal with long brown hair. It sings like a bird and can speak too. Nogorots are very sweet.'

'Can I come to your city?'

Arindata smiles.

'No. Your body isn't ready for space and time travel.'

'If you're the future, then what can I do now?' asks Jack. 'I can't change anything. The future will just happen.'

'No, Jack,' says Arindata. 'You can change the future in some ways. Your actions are very important. You must believe that. Now goodbye!'

Suddenly, Jack can't see Arindata and her city. And it's midnight on TV. Was it all a dream? He doesn't know. But now it's time to go to the party. It's time to see his friends. He wants to begin his future!

'I've come from the year 3000.'

How do you feel about

Answer these questions and find out.

1 Who did you spend Millennium night with?
a Your family   b Your boy/girlfriend   c Your friends

2 Where were you?
a At home   b At a party   c Out on the streets

3 What are you hoping for most in the new Millennium?
a World peace   b A better environment on our planet
c New discoveries in medicine and space

4 What is your idea of a great holiday in the future?
a Two weeks on a beach in the sun
b A month of travel and adventure
c A trip to the moon – or another planet

5 What do you think about history? Is it
a something that tells us about our past mistakes?
b full of interesting stories about people?
c something to forget – the future's more important?

6 What is your dream house of the future?
a Beautiful furniture, lots of rooms, big garden
b New and interesting, perhaps shaped like a dome
c No housework or cooking – all done by computer!

the new Millennium?

7 How would you like to travel in the future?
a In a safer, quieter kind of car
b In your personal plane
c As fast as possible. A spaceship, perhaps!

8 How do you see your work in twenty years' time?
a Easier, with more time for holidays
b Different – more interesting and more difficult
c Work? What work? The word is already history!

9 Which is the most important of these things for you?
a A long and healthy life
b Love and relationships
c Learning new things

10 What do you think about the new Millennium?
a You hope it won't bring too many changes.
b The future is worrying, but exciting too.
c You hope that soon everything will be different.

Now turn to Page 41.

Special Events for the Year 2000

Where is the best place to find out about the year 2000? Look on the Internet, if you can.

Here are some of the thousands of special events for the year 2000 in countries around the world.

FINLAND

A WALK THROUGH HELSINKI

The city of Helsinki is on the Internet! It's dark for weeks in Helsinki in winter. So it's not much fun going out. But now you can visit all the city streets and buildings on your computer.

You can 'walk' down the streets, and go into the shops and offices. You can even 'sit' in the theatre or listen to music shows.

IRELAND

A NEW ENVIRONMENT

Come to Ireland if you like walking! They are opening old country paths which the early Christians walked on long ago. In Dublin, they are planting new trees and building a new footbridge over the River Liffey.

CANADA

WALL OF PAINTINGS

The people of Canada are making a Great Millennium Wall with 2000 paintings in it.

NEW ZEALAND

A SECRET HIDING PLACE

They are building a special place for thousands of things from the year 2000. In it, they are putting photographs, films, things from people's homes, and machines and computers. They are closing it for a thousand years. 'Do not open!' says a sign. But in the year 3000, people will be able to learn about life in the year 2000.

RUSSIA

FROM MOSCOW TO JERUSALEM

Russia is sending twenty runners from Moscow to Jerusalem to celebrate 2000. They are also planning a large international meeting of young people to discuss world problems.

CHINA

A BIG JOB

The government of China is counting all the people in the country during the year 2000. This is a very big job!

AFRICA

SAVING THE EYES OF 20,000 PEOPLE

An international club, the Lions Club, has promised to save the eyes of 20,000 people every week of the new Millennium. Many people in Africa have eye problems which doctors can help. The club is giving money for the doctors.

UK

THE MILLENNIUM DOME, THE 'LONDON EYE', AND THE ROCK

People are visiting the Millennium Dome, by the River Thames in Greenwich, London. The Dome is 365 metres across and 100 metres high. Inside, there are fourteen zones. Each zone has a different subject – money, religion, journeys and our planet, Earth. In the Body Zone you can walk through the large body of a person. Another zone has a computer which makes your face fifty years older.

There is also a big new wheel in London, the British Airways 'London Eye'. It is opposite the Houses of Parliament, next to the River Thames, and it is 135 metres high. Fifteen hundred people can ride on the wheel every hour. There is a wonderful view of London from the top.

In Northern Ireland, a thousand young people are helping to put up a very large stone. It will stand 1000 centimetres high – one centimetre for each year of the new Millennium – and it will be the tallest stone in the UK.

USA

A VILLAGE ON THE PLANET MARS
Schoolchildren and students all over America are deciding how a hundred people can live on the planet Mars. They are planning a village there. They have to think how this village can really work. It needs good science, a good environment and teamwork. Of course, they can't really build this village on Mars – not yet! But it's fun thinking about it!

AUSTRALIA

OLYMPIC GAMES, SYDNEY 2000
More than 10,000 sportsmen and women from all over the world are arriving in Sydney for the international Olympic Games in September 2000. There are all kinds of sports there – horse-riding and sailing, running and weight-lifting, swimming and football.

The Olympic Games began in Greece a long time ago. The Games usually begin when a runner brings in the Olympic flame from Greece. But for the Millennium Games they are sending a flame out into space first. 'Space travel is important for our future – and it's international,' says one of the Olympic officers.

THE FUTURE

When the sun came up over Millennium Island in Kiribati in the Pacific on 1 January 2000, President Tito took a flame and passed it to a young man.

'Take this in hope and peace from Kiribati,' he said, 'so it can light up the world.'

But what kind of future will we have? Will there be peace in the world, or will there be more wars? Can we save our environment, or will we destroy our planet? Of course, we don't know the answers yet. But we must all think about these questions at the beginning of the new Millennium.

Some big changes

There have been great changes in the last thousand years:

	1000	**1900**	**2000**
World population	300,000,000	1,600,000,000	6,000,000,000
Difference between rich and poor countries	Less than 3 times as rich	10 times as rich	74 times as rich
Cars, lorries and buses on the road	None	50,000	650,000,000
Usual age of death	40	46 – 50	74 – 79
Number of babies who die in their first year		142 out of every 1,000	6 out of every 1,000

Some facts about life today

- ✘ The world is getting warmer. Traffic is one reason. This means that the seas will probably cover some of the lower areas of land.
- ✘ The population will double every forty years in the future. So the world will be very crowded.
- ✘ We are destroying more forests every day – we have lost 40% of the world's forests since 1970. This means that millions of animals and birds have lost their homes.

What's the good news?

- ✓ Most of the people in the world can now read and write.
- ✓ We have better medicine, and computers help us more in our work.
- ✓ At the end of 1999, scientists discovered a new 'Millennium Planet'. It is fifty 'light years' away in a group of stars that are called Bootis. Perhaps it will help us understand other planets. Perhaps we will even discover a planet with life on it, like our planet, Earth.
- ✓ For more than fifty years, people have been afraid of a new and terrible world war. But it hasn't happened. Perhaps we can believe that nobody really wants to destroy the world.

Hopes for the future

At the start of the new Millennium, many people in the world celebrated something together for the first time in history. Many of the celebrations were about peace.

In Rio de Janeiro, they tried to stop all shooting and fighting for seventy-two hours. Children there wrote down their hopes for peace. Many countries, like Russia, joined the 'One Day in Peace' event around the world.

A special place

In the Millennium Dome, in London, visitors can write their hopes for the new Millennium on a piece of paper. And at the centre of the zone for different religions in the Dome, there is a quiet, empty space. You can sit and think, and soft colours change slowly around you. Here we can remember that we are all different – but we are also the same. We are all people.

Changing times

In the modern world, changes are happening very fast. With changes in medicine, parents will soon be able to choose the kind of baby that they want. You will be able to change parts of your body if they don't work. You can make changes to your face too. So if you are old, you can still look young.

Our lives will be much, much longer. Soon, computers will be able to do more for us in our homes and at work. Perhaps we or our children will be able to travel to other planets and stars.

Some of these changes are exciting, and others are very frightening. And there will be other discoveries that we can't even dream about now.

Are we ready to meet them?

The way to the future

**For the new Millennium,
a group of Hopi American Indians put
a letter on to the Internet. It said:**

This is the time – this is the hour –
to think about these questions:
Where are you living?
What are you doing?
What relationships do you have?
Now do this:
Speak only what is true.
Make your own group of people.
Be good to other people.
Nobody can tell you what to do.
You can choose.
This can be a good time! The water in the river is moving fast now.
Some people are frightened. They try not to move. But the river is going somewhere.
Keep your eyes open and your head above water.
Swim!

ANSWERS

What do you know about times and dates?
Answers to questions on page 1

Give yourself 3 points for each correct answer.

1. c   1,000 years
2. a   Latin. It comes from *mille* (one thousand) and *annus* (year).
3. b   Time
4. c   We don't really know. Dionysius Exiguus started a new Christian calendar in the year 532. Christ was born on 25 December of the year before AD 1, he said. But he didn't use the number 0. Christ was born before King Herod died in 4 BC. He was probably born in 6 BC.
5. c   In the UK, in London.
6. a   Calculating international time. Since 1884, Greenwich has been the 'home of world time'.
7. b   The Pacific
8. b   One day earlier
9. c   Kiribati. The sun first came up over Caroline Island, one of the islands of Kiribati, and this island is now called Millennium Island.
10. b   6 p.m.

24 – 30 points
Very good! You already know a lot about times and dates. You are probably very interested in the Millennium.

15 – 21 points
You know a little, but you can learn more.

0 – 12 points
Don't you know anything about times and dates? Read this book now!

ANSWERS

How do you feel about the new Millennium?
Answers to questions on pages 30 – 31

Were most of your answers a, b or c?

Mostly a's
You like to feel safe and comfortable. You're more interested in the past than in the future. But you're sensible, and the new Millennium needs people like you!

Mostly b's
You're interested in events in the world around you, but relationships are more important to you. You'll enjoy the new Millennium. You can also give a lot to other people.

Mostly c's
You're off in your own spaceship already! You love the idea of change and a new Millennium. You have an open mind, but you need to come back down to earth sometimes.

ACTIVITIES

Pages 1 – 11
Before you read
1 Find these words in your dictionary. They are all used in this book.

bug calculate calendar celebrate dome firework flame god Internet millennium peace period planet predict prophecy zone

Which words can be about

a time?

b places?

c the future?

d parties?

e computers?

2 Discuss these questions.

a Why do people think that a new Millennium is special?

b How did you celebrate the start of this Millennium?

After you read
3 Answer these questions.

a How many calendars are in use in the world?

b In which country is the 'home of world time'?

c How many time zones are there in Russia?

d When and why did Kiribati move to the other side of the International Date Line?

4 Was your government worried about the Millennium Bug? What did they do about it? Were there any problems?

ACTIVITIES

Pages 12 – 23
Before you read
5 Talk about famous prophecies that you have heard or read about.
6 What are these sentences in your language?
   a There is a big musical *event* in the park this afternoon.
   b My *horoscope* says I'll be unlucky in love.
   c Do you have a good *relationship* with your parents?
   Now check the meanings of the words in *italics* in your dictionary.

After you read
7 Answer these questions about Story in the Stars.
   a Why is Nicky sad before the party?
   b Why is Alex so excited?
   c Why is Ingrid worried at the party?
   d What do Alex and Lela talk about?
8 Work with another student.
   Student A: You are Alex. Ask Lela about your future. Ask questions.
   Student B: You are Lela. Tell Alex about his future. Answer his questions.

ACTIVITIES

Pages 24 – 39
Before you read
9 Discuss how the world is changing in important ways. How is it better now than in the past? How is it worse? Will the future be better, do you think?

10 Find the word *environment* in your dictionary. Describe the environment of your home.

After you read
11 Jack asks Arindata, 'If you're the future, then what can I do now? I can't change anything. The future will just happen.' What do you think? Can each person's actions make a difference? Talk about people who have made great changes to the world in the past.

Writing
12 Choose a famous person and write a Millennium horoscope for them.

13 Describe a Millennium celebration in your country, or a special event for the year 2000.

14 You are a newspaper reporter. Ask the American students about their plans for a village on Mars. Write some questions and imagine their answers.

15 Write about your hopes for the new Millennium.

Answers for the Activities in this book are published in our free resource packs for teachers, the Penguin Readers Factsheets, or available on a separate sheet. Please write to your local Pearson Education office or to: Marketing Department, Penguin Longman Publishing, 5 Bentinck Street, London W1M 5RN.